Bernard Ashley

CITY LIMITS

STITCH-UP

ORCHARD BOOKS

ORCHARD BOOKS
96 Leonard Street, London EC2A 4RH
Orchard Books Australia
14 Mars Road, Lane Cove, NSW 2066
ISBN 1 86039 404 3 (hardback)
ISBN 1 86039 481 7 (paperback)
First published in Great Britain 1997
First paperback publication 1997
Text © Bernard Ashley 1997
The right of Bernard Ashley to be identified as the author of
this work has been asserted by them in accordance with the
Copyright, Designs and Patents Act, 1988.
A CIP catalogue record for this book is available from the
British Library.
Printed in Great Britain

Chapter One

It wouldn't be the same without the rumble of trains. Dean's place, 'City Limits'. You lived with a shake to things that could take a glass off a table if you weren't quick – thanks to City East Main Line, the station fifty metres down the road, its tracks in place of garden at the back.

Dean's place? It was his dad's snack bar; Dean's bedroom over the kitchen, where he could never get off to sleep if the trains ever stopped; timing his homework by the hourly to the East Coast. He was 'Dino' to his mates on account of his Italian mum and dad. And "Spag" to his enemies for the same reason – and he had some enemies, because he was one of those people who knew how many slices make a loaf of bread. On top of which, he was too quick and a bit loud – and he was blessed with the sort of face you find on an angel in a cemetery.

And, homework? It was way down the line compared to being around one of the tables in the snack bar, elbows and drinks on the marble, banging on about this and that with Mack, and Sharon, and anyone else who fancied hanging in. Which Renny didn't mind – that was Dean's dad, Renato – because if Dean was in here he knew where he was, and in the evenings there were always enough tables for the kids to have one of their own.

Tonight it was only Mack in City Limits with Dean. Mack, who was Dean's oldest friend from back in primary school. Mack, who didn't have a needle of Scottish blood in him, but got his name from always wearing this belt-up job in anything the wet side of drizzle. Mack, who was so City East he couldn't keep hold of an "h" if you glued it to his tongue; who'd had it hard, but lived now with his Auntie Pearl in a couple of rooms the other side of the railway. Mack, the true old mate, the *amico*.

Sharon was due in soon. It was Tuesday evening, and she'd said she'd come, after *The Simpsons*. Dean kept his eye on the KitKat clock on the wall, interested as he was in hearing how Auntie Pearl had lost her lighter and where Mack had come across it. Sharon was black and beautiful and a load of fun, and just seeing her smooth hands tapping the table, and not pulling away when he put his over hers, and her lifting his wrist to look at his watch as if she owned his arm, it gave him a buzz.

His dad was clearing out the display case, putting this deli dish into that, clearing the shelves for a fresh day tomorrow. At a table near the door a couple were staring through steaming tea into each other's eyes, knees held off touching by the suitcase between them. A young exec in a Top Man suit was on a stool in the window, enjoying his reflection, dipping bread into the egg of his all-day breakfast.

And Mack was going on a bit.

The door opened and Dean looked up, but not too snappy. You had to be mellow. It wasn't Sharon, though. It was a Chinese girl about the same age. And she was beautiful, like *beautiful*. And didn't Dean know her? It took a couple of looks and a bit of making sure.

"Wotcha Kwai," from Mack. He turned back to Dean. "It was only under that little bridge in the goldfish tank."

"What was?" Dean wasn't with him for a moment.

"This lighter she lost."

The girl was hovering, looking over at Renny – she'd got something to say to Renny, but she wasn't going to leave Dean out.

"Hello." She looked at him, direct, those eyes and that voice making the one word sound like Puccini.

He got up. "It's Kwai, isn't it?"

"What I said – it was Kwai," said Mack.

Dean checked the door. "You fancy a Coke?"

This was Kwai Ung, last seen at St George's Primary School, Year Six, before she went to the All Hallows Girls' High, while most of the rest of them had gone to Barbican Comprehensive. And had she changed? At St George's she'd been small and quiet, the one you never picked for anything. A year at All Hallows and all sorts had happened – the sort of all sorts that suddenly put the knock on Dean's hand and had his Coke over, fizzing across the table and all down one leg.

"Trains!" he said, while Renny threw a cloth at his head.

"Wick all wet," Mack said, relentless.

Dean shot him a puzzled look and then got going with the cloth.

"The wick on the lighter."

"What I've come for–" Kwai had gone over to Renny, who was coming round from behind the display case. She took a note from her waist bag and handed it to him. "It's this."

Renny read it like a collector with a paint-ing – both hands, arms length, like steering something. "No problem." He gave the paper a finger slap, handed it back to her; it could have been hard currency. "You boys, come on!"

Dean finished wiping. Mack was up already – Renny was good to Mack in the way of drinks and doughnuts – while Kwai started explaining to the men on the move.

"My dad's Coke order didn't come. He hoped you could help."

"We got plenty." Dean had the boss's voice, was about to click his fingers at his dad. "How many do you want?"

"I said no problem, relax and take it easy." Renny opened the door to the back where soft drinks and paper napkins went up the stairs. "You take a hold of this, and this." He pulled off three cases of twenty-four. Dean and Mack hoisted them, tried to make them look light, nearly put themselves in A&E up at the Royal Free.

"Have you got wheels outside?" Dean asked.

"No, he'll come round..." Kwai said.

But Renny wasn't having that. Not with two strong layabouts laying about. "My boys'll walk it round," he said. And from the passage he trundled the porters' barrow, still branded *BR City East*.

"You want me to sign for these?" Kwai asked.

"Why, are you going to run away to China?" Renny shook his head. "Pay back when your delivery comes. No problem."

"Where are we going?" Dean wanted to know. He *seriously* wanted to know.

"The Golden Buddha," she told him. "Not far."

Which it wasn't, he knew it now, but he'd never tied it in with Kwai Ung.

He took the barrow handles, the big man. "OK," he said, and had to jump twice to swing his weight enough for lift off. "Get a good grip..."

Renny held the door for him, and Dean had just a flash of a thought to ask him to say a "sorry" to Sharon, tell her he wouldn't be more than the flap of a bee's wing. But he left it. She'd be OK, no sweat.

"I'll get 'er a new one for Christmas," Mack told Kwai.

"A new what?" She stepped in next to him, behind Dean and the barrow.

"A new lighter. My Auntie Pearl."

"Ah," Kwai said. "Very kind."

Chapter Two

Back in City Limits, Top Man finished his meal and peeled off a note to pay, not a word, top macho stuff. Too much staring at himself had given him a sad case of the Robert de Niros. *Stupido!* But Renny kept a serious face; he wanted customers back again, so he corked his laugh. His little stock room was filled with saved-up laughs: he dived in there sometimes like a man busting to spend a *piastre*.

He looked across at the sad Romeo who

was doing the balcony scene over his suitcase, but Juliet was dabbing her nose with a paper napkin, snuffling, so Renny got on with his clearing up – no little chat over there.

This was a good time of day. Mornings he worked like someone with four hands, slicing, buttering, filling; turning this, whisking that; frothing, spooning, grilling, blending; plating, serving, washing, racking – till by lunch time he was sometimes meeting himself the other side of the counter, coming back. *Grazie a Dio*, afternoons ran down a bit; time for a look at the paper.

There may be a spurt of catch-the-train-home trade, but around now was when he might flick a 2B out of his apron pocket and sketch a face that had taken his eye. A skinny city beauty or a lively look twinkling out of some crumpled paper bag of a face. And if he wasn't in the artistic mood he'd wipe over the celebs he'd drawn as a young waiter in Monte Carlo, and dream of being young again, in the Mediterranean sun.

Unless Sharon came in. Which she did right now. Nothing else went on in your head when Sharon was about. She filled every space going. There was no room for dreaming *and* for Sharon Ross. She was loud, bright, funny, had you on the twist of her wrist. You could be walking in Parliament Square and, if Sharon were with you, you wouldn't hear Big Ben.

She was known and noted as Dean's girl-friend; and no harm in that, Renny reckoned. It was if she ever went quiet; that's when he'd worry. She'd got a trace of make-up on her lips, and her hair was pretty in pink ribbons to match. He could see why his boy was all over the place about her.

"What time you got, Renny?" Busy, busy,

busy. She slumped across two chairs and wiped the table with her elbow, flashing gum out of her pocket.

Renny eyed up at the clock. "Look, and you shall see."

She sat up again. "So where's Dino Strychnino? I've got a meeting down the road, top of the clock."

"He's doing a favour for me."

"What sort of favour? Left the country, please God."

"Delivery. Won't be long."

Angelica must have heard Sharon come in. City East must have heard Sharon come in. Dean's ten-year-old sister slipped herself up on a chair next to the girl, for the action.

"An-gel eyes!"

The hand slapping they did was more like dance steps. And within ten seconds two Cokes and a saucer of pistachios were on the table.

"You're the top stack, Renny."

"Call it Dean's wages, for the favour."

The sad couple went, the suitcase heavy and pulled on small wheels. Renny opened the door for them.

"*Grazie*, come again."

The man muttered something.

"He's headin' back to his wife!" Sharon sucked on her straw. "What my dad never done. He stuck with us – Mum and me."

"Ssssh!" Renny shut the street door. But City Limits was empty of customers now.

"Written all over his face." She sucked her Coke. "One straw for two bottles. It don't last long."

"Well, that's for them, eh?"

Angelica cracked a pistachio. "How do you know?" she asked Sharon.

"You always know when a dog's got the guilts. They look at you so loving."

At which Angelica nodded wisely, and Renny shook his head. So quickly, children grew up these days.

Wesley Road was busy. City commuters walked bent and fast towards the station. The roadway was a congealed line of cars and taxis and buses. All of which made pushing three cases of heavy Cokes seem like steering a pram along a mountain path.

Dean was soon ready for a swap with Mack – and not just because of the sweat of it. Mack and Kwai were strolling along behind like a couple of *capos*, talking old mate stuff; which shouldn't have made him jealous, him with a girlfriend. But it did.

"You want a go on this, Mack?"

"No, ta, mate."

"Mack!"

"What, you cream-crackered already?"

"'Course not." Dean couldn't be sure, but was Mack holding Kwai's hand? Baloney! He wasn't the sort, old Mack.

"I'll push it," Kwai said. "It's our delivery. I'm sorry to be a pain."

Dean had stopped now, was standing by the barrow like a porter waiting while someone found their two quid. But the pavement was on a narrow city street, and a stream of heart-cases were getting hampered and huffy as they tried to push past. It was a tall beauty in a business suit and high heels who spoke for them all in her clipped, posh voice.

"Get out of the stuffing way!"

Dean pulled over against the building, next to a Nat West hole-in-the-wall. He ignored the sweet-talking tall beauty and gave two big Italian eyes to Kwai, in a look which was not going to blink before she did.

"It's no sweat. I could push this to Hong Kong. It's just... it's my turn to walk next to you."

Kwai stared back at him, dropped her mouth open to show her white, even teeth, while Mack yooped and turned to kick the Nat West wall. "You smooth ratbag!"

A forty-something slicker in a striped suit was getting a tune out of the cash dispenser, tapping in his PIN. He looked round and missed a digit at this uncouth language which was creasing his jacket. He tried again, all Mack's fault. Mack took the barrow handles off Dean.

"Give it 'ere, Mary Ann."

"No, I'm—"

The striped suit was laying hands upon a wad of notes, like taking toast from a baby's mouth. Dean and Mack were tussling at the barrow handles, Dean easing round to let Mack win and get himself next to Kwai. When from somewhere in the slugstream of traffic a figure came arcing in on roller blades. Long black coat, black woollen hat pulled down, leather slickwrist gloves. He jumped the kerb, came in on a fast curve, and without braking or colliding, snatched the cash from Striped Suit's fingers in a flash precision flick.

"Oi!" The loser suddenly sounded more East End than City. "Oi! Come back! You thieving beggar!"

But the in-liner was already a lamp post away, getting air over the back wheel of a motorbike and speed skating in and out of the traffic.

"You see that?"

"The tyke!"

"Ye gods! Is nothing safe any more?"

The pavement had suddenly congealed

with people, disgusted, shocked, outraged, angered.

"How much have you lost?" someone asked.

"Too much!" Striped Suit said.

"Is there a policeman anywhere?"

"Is there ever a policeman when you want one?"

Everyone was disgusted, shocked, outraged and angered all over again.

"'E came like a bat out of 'ell!" Mack said.

Striped Suit looked Mack up and down. "You're right," he said. "The black trash!"

Chapter Three

Striped Suit slid out his card once more, did a quick mental take-away with his overdraft. He put the plastic into the machine again and played the tune he'd played before. But this time the toast was a thinner slice.

"Did you know him?" Striped Suit looked between the kids and chose Dean, as if he might be the one giving the most chance of a straight answer.

"No way!"

"He knew what he was doing! Too well! That was a practised move."

"It was skill, I'll go along with that."

"You admired it, did you?"

"Listen – 'ave you got a problem with us?" Mack wasn't one to let words dance around without their feet touching the ground some-time.

"No. I'm trying to... I have just lost a lot of money. I've had a nasty shock."

"An' I'm sorry for that. But don't you start taking it out on us. Right?"

The man held his hands up like a footballer apologising for a kick up someone's rear.

"We're witnesses, if you want us." Dean felt in his pocket for one of Renny's City Limits cards.

But Striped Suit waved it away. "It's already written off to experience."

"But you're going to report it, aren't you?"

"Oh, yes?" The man patted his pockets, buttoned his jacket, straightened himself and took a fresh grip on his briefcase. "Trains to Norwich run on the half-hour, I want to get home some time tonight."

"Well, if I'd lost a small fortune, I'd want to report it," Dean said.

"It wasn't a *small fortune*," Striped Suit snapped. "No need to go over the top..."

Dean looked at him hard. The man had one of those could-be-young, could-be-middle-aged faces; pale eyes with light eyelashes which gave him a stare. His mouth looked as if it could spit as well as talk. Fancy being the one waiting for him in Norwich, with his din-dins in the oven! Let the beggar lose his dosh, if he felt like that.

"Why waste my time, why waste police time?" the man was going on. "Black crime's so common the police have given up on it.

No-go areas, *their* streets. The second I describe that lout, you'll see the policeman close his eyes like pulling down a shutter."

Dean was glad that Mack had hold of the barrow. It left his hands free to stop this guy walking off.

"Hang on," he said. Inside, his stomach had gone electric. The knock of what this nerd had said had hit Dean as if he'd been saying it about Sharon.

The man looked down at Dean's hand on his sleeve. Dean lifted it.

"Who says black crime is worse than the rest? And are all the victims white? Who says the police have given up on *any* form of crime?"

"Come on, son, it's a known fact."

"Only in the *Daily Nazi*."

"And I have a train to catch." Striped Suit wanted away now, he was getting in too deep.

"I feel sorry for you, mate," Mack put in. "Sorry you lost your dosh – an' sorry you fall for all that fascist rubbish. I'm a kid – am I supposed to look up to the likes of you?"

"You can look wherever you like. I'm only stating known facts. As it happens, I've got some very good coloured friends..."

Dean just laughed in his face. This was so predictable it was like playing solo whist with a see-through deck. "You know what?" he said. "Given you don't get your dosh back, I hope that guy gets a bit of *joy* out of it. It might make up just a little bit for all the stick he's had to take from people like you."

"So you do know him?"

"Sort of," he said. "I'm Italian. I don't get the skin thing, but I get a ton of the rest. Oh, yeah – I know some of his grief."

Kwai was nodding. She knew some of his grief, too. "Don't waste our time," she said.

And she took the barrow handles herself, leaving Dean and Mack to walk behind and spit swearwords about the man in the striped suit. Until Dean came to, and made Mack take over. But his walk with Kwai wasn't the nice relaxed little chat he'd thought it would be. Their blood was all too fizzed up for that.

Dean had been past The Golden Buddha often enough, it had never stopped him though. It wasn't a place you could gawp into because it had a black window with just a menu in the middle. Up-market was the word for it.

True to all that, Kwai wasn't going to let them trolley a delivery through the front door. She led them down an alley to where the side door was protected by a hanging New Year lantern.

Her father must have seen them coming through the black of the window. He opened up and smiled at Mack, who had got himself in front.

"Renny says no problem," Mack said. "Pay back when your delivery comes."

Dean wanted to give Mack a shove in the back. *He* was the City Limits son, not this long streak of jellied eel. But Kwai pulled him forward. Good old, beautiful Kwai.

"This is Dean Romita. City Limits. And this is Mack Collins. Both friends from the old school."

"Hello. And thank you."

Mack smiled like a Reception child being given a second biscuit. Not many people remembered him enough to keep a hold on his other name.

Kwai said something to her father in Cantonese. He was nodding and smiling at

Dean, so it had to be something about the arrangements for repaying the Cokes.

"End of the week," he confirmed. He took the top case off the barrow and put it in the inside passage. Mack fell over himself to be the one with the next, and Dean made sure he wasn't left out on the third.

"And, please take," Kwai's father said. From nowhere he produced a bag of prawn crackers.

Mack thanked him – as *he* took it. He turned to Kwai, who was looking at Dean with a serious stare. "I was wondering. You wanna come out? I mean, come back for a Coke at our place?"

Our place? Dean looked up at the slit of sky he could see from the alley. But it seemed as if God wasn't looking down so small a crack.

Because Kwai was giving that special sort of look to Mack now. "Yes, please!" she said. A little girl being offered a tutti-frutti ice-cream.

And Dean looked back down the alley to the street. A look away. Sharon would be in City Limits when they got there. His girl-friend. Special, funny, beautiful Sharon.

So why was he standing there feeling jealous?

Chapter Four

Renny had found something to do in the back room. Sharon had just about burned the hands off the KitKat clock, looking up at it with her fiery eyes. And if she asked him, "Where?" once, she asked him ten times. "Are we talking The Golden Buddha round the corner, or up in Manchester?"

If a customer had come in, Renny would have held the cup to their lips, buttered their toast for them, sprinkled their supper with salt and pepper, grain by grain – anything to take his mind off the vibes of that girl being kept waiting.

And when Dean did come in with Kwai, and Mack third through the door, Renny wanted to get down behind his counter and crawl away. The little *buffone*, hadn't he got any sense? The boy opened the door like a royal flunkey, bowed Kwai in as if she were the pearl of the East – kept Mack back with his foot – and said, "There you go!" like showing off the house he'd built for her.

At the first click, Sharon's eyes had locked on to that door. And before Dean was fully up from his bow she was on her feet with her chair flat on the floor behind her.

"You been to Bangkok, or what?"

"Hey! Hey!" Dean opened his arms at Sharon like a ringmaster celebrating the flying trapeze. "Teaching Mack how to show a lady in," he said, sharp as a bee sting. "Treat the lady *like* a lady!"

Mack gave him a look to peel wallpaper, and Renny had Cokes on the table before Sharon's chair was up off the floor. But Mack needed no prompts from Dean.

"'Ere, y'are, Kwai." He pulled her out a chair and sat it in beneath her. Which was spoiled just a bit by him trapping her knee against the table leg.

Angelica looked up at the four older kids. She guzzled into her second Coke, burped on it, and put her chin in her hands, her elbows on the table. She was learning how to hang out.

But Sharon left her drink to fizz itself off. She looked at Mack, she looked at Dino Strychnino, the soul brother, who was looking at her so loving. And she looked at Kwai, who was taking all night chasing the straw with her mouth, eyes on the job.

"Are you the person I think you are?" Sharon asked Kwai.

"What person do you think I am?"

"That kid from St George's. You was to talking what I was to keeping stumm."

Angelica finished her drink with a snort. Dean and Mack laughed at the noise as if Oscar Wilde had delivered a shaft of wit. It was getting sticky in City Limits. Renny reached for a plate of *pasticceria*, to clam up some mouths.

"I talk when I've got stuff to say." Kwai somehow made it sound polite. And her eyes, her tightened nose, her chin up said she'd got something to say right now. "I think you did well, Dean, with what you said to that man outside the bank."

"What man?" Sharon wanted to know.

"'E done terrific," Mack said. "Told *'im*!"

And Mack thumped the table the way he'd attacked the bank wall.

Quickly, Dean filled Sharon in with the roller blade robbery. And Mack smoothed it off with how Dean had stuck up for city blacks.

"I'll tell the brothers an' the sisters." Sharon didn't sound impressed, the way people never do who weren't in on the action.

"I think you were great," said Kwai. And she blinked her eyelids slowly, the look someone might give while they're being kissed.

"Anyhow, Great One, I've got a meet with Clyde." Sharon reached across the table and lifted Mack's wrist to see the time. But Mack wasn't a watch wearer. Dean was, but she resorted to the KitKat on the wall.

Dean beat her to her feet. Inside, he felt as if he'd guzzled *all* their Cokes; down there things were erupting like hot springs. "Clyde?

That's your brother, isn't it?" he asked, showing great interest.

"You wanna meet him?" Sharon asked. "Could you rip yourself out of here?"

Dean's hands said it all. "Could I *not*!" He got to the door and held it for her.

But, "Nothing tarty for me!" Sharon said, and whipped herself through it before he could make the start of a bow.

Chapter Five

They'd done up City East station. The pillars had been cleaned back to their old Portland stone, Europlants had made the place look like a nursery, and the concourse reflected beneath people's feet.

"Not a place to walk in a skirt!" Sharon always said.

Not that Sharon was a rail traveller. But like the rest of City East she used the place for late shopping, and for meeting up. Travellers Fare and the rest sold most of everything you wanted. And there were half-comfortable seats, and that buzzy feel of people on the move. You just didn't want to look a scruff, meeting up, that was all, or the railway Old Bill would move you on as a downer.

She walked in ahead of Dean. Tonight, the mood was off the boil for holding hands, somehow. Which would be down to Kwai, Dean reckoned. And this Clyde meeting.

Clyde was Sharon's half-brother. He lived somewhere up the road with his mother, while Sharon lived at home with their dad and her own mother. Dean had never met him before, but he know about the boy and how he gave his mum the runaround.

Sharon found a couple of seats. Dean took one, to keep it for Clyde.

"I'll—" he started.

"Yeah, you fade when he comes."

Fade? Cheers! If it hadn't been for how bad he felt over Kwai, Dean wouldn't have come at all. But he *did* feel bad. He'd felt bad in City Limits and he hadn't stopped feeling bad all along the street. Or was *guilty* the word? Because he'd betrayed Sharon, in his head. He'd had little thoughts that he shouldn't have had.

His old heart had put on a bit of a spurt when Kwai had looked at him. And when she'd congratulated him for what he'd said to that man, he'd had a tingle where he shouldn't have had a tingle. And, OK, he wasn't married to Sharon, but everyone at school knew not to muscle between Dino and Sha. They were an *item*. Now he was trotting along trying to be her best friend.

She sat there staring around, rapping her fingers to some tune going on in her head.

"What are you seeing him for?" Dean

dared to ask. Well, he'd have asked yesterday —
so why feel pokey about asking today?

But Sharon answered like yesterday, which
unhooked him from his spike, just a bit.

"He owes Dad. Some fee or something for
a course. Now he ain't doing the course so
he's got to give it back." She kept her eyes rov-
ing for this Further Ed failure to show. "He'd
better come, or the old man's going round for
it — an' then there'll be the riots all over!"

Dean looked at Sharon.

"We're talking a couple of big ones, that's
why. For a photography course. He had to put
in for the gear."

Dean was still nodding when Clyde suddenly arrived; came among them from out of
nowhere.

"Sister blister, give me some!"

"Big bad brother!"

They didn't kiss, but smacked skin.

Dean could see the family connection, even the half. Clyde had the same shape to his face, and a nose you could have switched, his for hers. Perhaps just a meaner pair of eyes.

And a long black coat. And a head that only needed a black woollen hat to make him seem like someone Dean knew. From earlier that night, from outside the back, being the same size, as he was...

And Dean didn't say "Hi!" straight off because he was looking down at Clyde's trainers. Scruffy, off-white, the way most were. But with pinches in the welts where old skates might grip.

"See you!" Dean said to Sharon. And from under his arm, "Hi!" to the tall guy, as he tried to melt away fast into a dwarf palm.

Chapter Six

It would have taken a double saint not to keep eyes on Clyde and Sharon. Dean edged his backside onto a seat behind the fronds of the palm and fished out his *i-d* to study; his eyes focused way past it on Bro and Sis. And what he saw bubbled the fizz inside him worse than ever.

OK, he knew Clyde was there to give over with either cash or excuses – and it was cash, as it happened. But the *style* of the cash was what gave Dean the dry mouth. It was neat cash, new notes, folded slim, like the crisp stuff that Striped Suit had taken out of the machine. And it was handed over at the speed of light, as if it could have been dosh for dope.

Oh, God! Why was life so tricky? Why did it keep putting you on the line? Why did you have to get the sweats about feeling a bit special over more than one girl? And why did out-of-line people have to skate so near to your own front door?

The bank notes were in Sharon's pocket now, and Bro and Sis were getting up. The deal was done. And the way this Clyde was looking around and edging his feet away, he wasn't hanging about to catch up on any family news.

Dean came out of Kew Gardens and drifted back to Sharon, his hand out to take her arm and help the move away from Clyde. But it was on exactly the same shake as someone else homing in from their other side. Striped Suit – who was pointing at Clyde and leading a female Old Bill.

The nerd must have missed his train and decided that Dean had been right – he *should* report the robbery. And he had.

"This is the guy," he told the WPC.

Clyde stared down at him. "What guy's that, man?"

"You know very well."

Clyde looked at Sharon, laughed, swung his head from side to side like a bored tiger. "I know very well *what*?"

"Hang on." The WPC twisted her neck downwards and did some police-speak into her radio.

Back-up, Dean thought. Reinforcements. City East nick pouring out into meat wagons, stopping only to sign for their Smith and

Wessons. And here he was standing next to Suspect Number One. If he tried to drift away a bit casual they'd probably put out an all ports alert.

"And he was there, too." Now Striped Suit was pointing at Dean.

He said nothing. Well, he had been there, hadn't he?

A little crowd was gathering now – the sort who liked street theatre but would never sling a penny in the hat.

"Let's get this clear." The WPC was standing firm between Clyde and Striped Suit, and her voice was even-steven between the two of them, not on one side and not on the other. Yet...

"You're accusing this young man of stealing cash from your hand..."

"'Young man'!" Clyde went down laughing. Dean looked at Sharon, shook his head.

He reckoned Clyde should have done the laugh on "stealing" if he wanted off the hook.

"...And you've just seen him hand over cash to this young woman."

Now Sharon burst. By the looks of her, she'd been waiting for the right point to burst. "This *young woman* is his sister, and this *young man* has just given me some money he owes our father. And if you want to check on that, you can come to my place and see our dad."

"She said it," Clyde added. "That money come from my mattress." He stretched his hand out to Sharon. "Show it," he said. "That ain't stolen money. That's two hundred and five pounds off our old man which I kept 'cos I didn't use it. For a course I never done."

Sharon produced the cash. But it still looked shiny new.

Striped Suit's neck was doing the giraffe. "So what is there on this to say it came from under your bed and not out of my bank machine?"

Someone in the little crowd peered forward, perhaps on the look-out for a bit of bed fluff.

"I dunno. That's where it come from. What's there to say it didn't?" Now Clyde breathed in heavy, and Dean could see the look of a guy starting to get angry, who would have poked his fingers in Striped Suit's chest if the WPC hadn't been standing between them. As it was, he was just about over her shoulder. "An' if you want to call some shots down the pig sty, let's get down there right now."

"Hang on." The WPC had her notebook out. "What time was this theft?" she asked Striped Suit.

And Mr Efficient had out his transaction ticket. "Eighteen thirty-seven."

"So where were you, Sir, at eighteen thirty-seven?" she asked Clyde.

It came out, straight off. "I was with her, Sharon Ella Ross." He looked at Sharon, who looked at him. "Before I scooted off to get the dosh."

"*Scooted*? He means before he *skated*!" Striped Suit looked as if he might splatter the station with an exploded head. "And I told you *he* was there!" Now his road-rage face was boiling at Dean.

"Yeah, I was there. At the bank. On a message for *my* dad, taking some Cokes to The Golden Buddha. Passing by." Dean didn't know that injustice could so rob your mouth of the skill of speaking. His voice sounded like a strangled parrot. "I told you to report it, didn't I – an' you gave me an argument, over Old Bill never doing anything about black crime!"

"Are you putting words in my mouth?"

"And where were you?" the WPC asked Sharon.

"At his dad's place. City Limits."

"With your brother?"

"Like he said."

Oh, no! Dean wanted to turn three hundred and sixty degrees. Then he wanted to be home in bed, dreaming all this. Holy cats! She was putting herself right in it now!

"We was sorting the stock out the back, while Dino went to The Golden Buddha."

"And you're Dino?"

Dean nodded.

"Is what she says right?" the WPC asked him, straight.

There was a silence over the whole world. Trains were being announced, music was playing, people were talking and calling. But for Dean there was the silence that drops like a rope noose around a lie.

"Just like she says."

"Well, I'm on at ten tomorrow," the WPC told them. "I'll take some names and addresses now. And I'll call in to see your father in the morning." This for Dean, not Sharon. "He'll be there?"

Dean nodded. He had now lost the skill of speech altogether.

"It's a stitch-up!" Striped Suit said.

And while no one rose to that, Dean knew he was right. Because who was being stitched up? Dino Antonio Romita.

Chapter Seven

Striped Suit ran for the late train to the sticks. Waddled, more like – like a toddler with a nappy full. But the smell around the platform wasn't down to him. It was down to Clyde.

"Cheers, man. That's appreciated."

The WPC had noted names and addresses: she had listed the serial numbers on the money Sharon was holding, and gone. The little crowd had drifted off once no one had had to assume the position. So, unless the palms in the station pots were bugged, Bro, Sis and Dino weren't being ear-holed.

"What is all that?!" Sharon said it for Dean. She said it the way people speak when they're hacking at someone's shins. "You weren't down no City Limits! What are you dishing up, man?"

Clyde answered like an innocent guy. Clever, Dean reckoned. "Because I wasn't *nowhere* at that time he's got on his little ticket. I was driftin' about. I was here, I was there. No one can't give me an out..."

"Your mum knew you had the dosh. She could say. Or was she driftin' about, an' all, here an' there?"

Clyde shook his head. "She never knew I got the notes in the first place. She would've wopped me good if she knew I went to the man for big dosh like that. If she couldn't raise it, she wouldn't want me doin' it."

Sharon clicked her mouth at him, the noise for when she couldn't find the words.

"That's why I never done the stupid course! I couldn't keep up no lie with her over no two years."

"Be the first time you couldn't keep up a lie!" Sharon turned away. "You dropped Dino Strychnino here *right* in it."

Clyde came back to Dean, where he'd started. "It's appreciated, Dino. You're bright, you'll think of something."

Dean wished he'd been big enough to give this guy one in the guts. "I'm thinking about my dad. Tomorrow, when the Old Bill come in. You're making me an accessory after the crime..."

"Like I said, you'll think of something."

"In your dreams!"

"But I'm innocent, man!"

Dean stared up at the big fella, as Sharon sidled up to him and ran her fingers down his arm, held his hand, laced up, their special way.

"If Dino gets his old man to tell lies, it ain't for you, Clyde Ross," she told her brother. "It's for me. Because we're an item. That's for who."

"For *anyone*. I'm grateful."

Sharon squeezed fingers. "An' we are an item, right, Dino?"

Her eyes were big, her lips were beautiful; it was only that 'just checking' look they had on them. Was he being put to some test?

"Yeah, we're an item," he said. His only complaint being, he felt like the sort of shoddy item that gets kicked into the gutter.

Dean stared at Juventas on his bedroom door. How could anyone be smiling at a time like this? OK, the hard men at the back weren't creasing their mouths, but all the young *atletas* were grinning at the camera like Saturday morning telly. He lay on his bed and twisted into his twentieth new position, the sheets about a day behind. It might be all right in grinning Turin, but City East was the pits of a place to be tonight.

Kwai was out of the picture now; he reckoned he'd forgotten Kwai – Mack had all Dino's blessings for a sweet romance in that direction. But, how the hell was he going to square his dad? That was the gristle stuck in his teeth. Because he knew his dad wasn't someone who *anybody* squared. In Dean's eyes, when people talk big about being their own man, they're modelling themselves on Renny Romita. He was a man who'd upped and done his own thing.

After Nonno Romita died, Renny's share in his father's Monte Carlo *ristorante* hadn't earned itself a lire's interest before he was in London looking to set up on his own. Forget Art School, forget sending his work to the Ad Agencies in the hope of a start, Renny loved Sophia Piana, and if he didn't marry her quick, he'd lose her.

And London was where the money was, and where business people had to eat. So Malone's Railway Caff became City Limits, the best of British and continental mouthfuls; fair prices, good feel – and no credit: it didn't matter who, if they didn't have the bread, they didn't eat the pastries.

A guy peddling protection had once come in, was going to look after Renny in the way of fire, vandalism, nasty accidents, all those sorts of things – some East End Charlie dropping big crook names. But Renny had sided the counter like the east wind round a corner, held the door, dropped his voice and croaked *Mafia* in his thickest Sicilian take-off. Charlie hadn't come back.

No, you didn't square Renny: not even Dean could do that. Renny had to want to do it himself.

And why should he want to lie to the police for Clyde Ross?

Chapter Eight

Below Dean's bedroom window the last rumble of train had gone east and the last shunt had put itself into the sidings. While, in his bed and out of it, Dean had gone every way round how he could get Renny wearing the same team shirt as him and Sharon. His mouth was dry with the talking in his head, his shoulders ached with the hunching in the mirror. He had addressed the jury, approached the bench, been cross-examined. And coming back at him he'd had the head shake, the calm chat, the sermon, the shout. His dad's hands had talked, rested, gone on buttering, held his shoulder, blessed his head.

Dean had skinned everything so thin that the light shone through. And what did he see, by the time his brain was on the verge of sacking out? He saw what it would all hang on. Every argument, every twist — whether Renny's door swung open or shut — would all hang on the one hinge.

Sharon.

It would all hang on the way Renny felt about Dean and Sharon. If Renny bought Sharon, he might just buy Clyde — for her sake. If he didn't, Dean could forget any alibi, any favours.

His burned out head had hardly touched the pillow when he found himself back downstairs in the snack bar...

There were no customers in; it was empty, apart from Renny. And Renny was doing what he liked doing at those times, sitting at a table with a sketch pad in front of him, right now colouring-in with Angelica's crayons some portrait he'd done – which Dean couldn't see from where he was standing. He was working fast – good artists always worked like cooks at a cucumber, Dean reckoned. Himself? He took six school art lessons to sketch a straight line.

Right now, he came over to Renny's table, watched him holding the portrait out to check what he was doing – and he heard him giving it his thoughts about the subject.

"*Bella!* The eyes, the nose." He turned to Dean. "You know what, you're a lucky *figlio* to be friends with this girl."

Dean nodded, smiled, and caught his face in the mirror looking *so* smug. But it was true,

Sharon was class fixings. He always felt real swank when it was Dino Romita who walked in with her through the classroom door.

And the rest! Dean stopped like someone put on "pause". This alibi door was swinging open, wasn't it? If Renny was doing Sharon's picture and going on this way about her, wasn't there a good chance he'd give her brother the "out"? Wasn't this just what Dean had wanted? Couldn't he harp on the tears going to come into those beautiful brown eyes if he didn't? Couldn't he talk about the shame for Sharon, and the knock-on shame for him?

This was the nearest he was likely to get to a strike, wasn't it?

Renny still had the Michaelangelo look on his face as Dean went over, gearing himself up to go for it. He heard his voice in his head doing a run at what he was going to say. He felt his heart starting to pump him up for the job. But he walked as casually as he could over to his dad and angled the picture to himself, to agree with the good things the man had been saying. Just for openers.

Clunk! It wasn't Sharon at all. It was Kwai. Kwai Ung, looking up at him like a dream...

There were no words now. Just a gulp and a thick clear of the throat. Which was when the street door opened and a customer came in. But no one after a bite – more like, someone on the snatch. It was Clyde Ross; and not on his soles but in a pair of shiny red Oxygen roller blades, ankle hugging and strapped up the leg. He came in at speed like the thief in the street, shot arcing round a table on the cutting edge of the wheels, heelbraked by Renny – and grabbed the picture from Renny's hands.

"What you playing at...?"

But Clyde hadn't got the speed up to take

him back through the door before Dean was there, blocking his way.

"Give that back, you great two-timer!"

"Out the way, man. This poster's mine." He tried to lay one on Dean, but it's hard to fight on roller blades, the feet don't hold. Clyde had left himself open to a push which sent him crashing across into a table, and dumping down onto a chair.

"Give that here!" Dean was grabbing at the picture – with no danger of tearing it because somehow it was now in a solid frame.

Not that Clyde was sitting there while coffee came. He launched himself off, crouched like someone going to jump for air, and went for the door.

"Can't do my photography, Dino, I got to have something snappy to flash the eye at."

"Me, too! That's for me!" Dean did a slide of his own, came in low, feet first, snatched the frame from Clyde's hands – while Renny ran to the door, threw it wide open and took Clyde by his neck and his bum and gave him to the street.

The door was shut fast.

"Santa Maria!" Renny said. Which was all.

Dean got to his feet and held the picture to his chest. He ran with it out of the snack bar and up to his room, shaking on the outside and trembling on the in. He went direct to the wall above his bed where an empty hook was waiting for the picture.

Hot-eyed and still heaving from the fight, Dean put the portrait where he could see it; stood back to take it in.

The portrait of Sharon, looking *bella*. Not Kwai anymore, but the beautiful Sharon. They were frightening, confusing, mixed-up things, dreams.

Chapter Nine

Compared to the dream, the real talk with Renny was well down on the action front, but still pretty high on the drama.

Renny opened up City Limits at half seven for the sparrows – cleaners coming out of the offices and the humpers and lumpers going in – all too poor to spend much, just after cups of sweet tea and the odd slice of toast. It was while the *Gaggia* coffee machine snorted and the bread browned that Renny buttered and filled and served, while Dean's mother made the salads and set out the deli.

But he was always up and ready for six o'clock, listening to *City Today* by the blue light of the fly sizzler, bringing in the bread and milk, wiping the overnight city dust off the tables; a quiet time on his own which never changed, except the getting older, day by day.

It ran against life's juices for Dean to be about that early. If it weren't for school, Dean's day would begin when the sun was well up and dressed. But this morning he pulled himself out of his sheets just after six, splashed his face, and in his shorts and tee shirt crept barefoot downstairs like a Cherokee brave — to have pow-wow with Big Chief before rest of tribe awoke.

He found Renny looking out through the wall of window, staring at life going past, the traffic which even this early couldn't have raced a dolls' pram. His dad turned round to Dean in the doorway, put his head on one side.

"You got a problem," he said. *Said*, didn't ask.

Cherokee brave nodded.

Renny waved his hand at a table and went to the *Gaggia* to make it snort two cups of *espresso*. Dean sat where he always sat, but it didn't feel like his corner this morning. There were the same patterns on the marble, but they were the background to his hands laid flat, not to the lean of his elbows.

"So – what's the headache you got?"

Dean couldn't look up at Renny's face. He didn't want to see the worry which had to be there – was the boy going to be expelled from school, had he done something stupid with Sharon? It was too easy, his dad's voice.

"It's Clyde. Sharon's brother."

Dean saw Renny relax, by a millimetre's move of the hand on the table. But he saw it tense again as he launched into his story; the tale of the trip with the Coke, the snatch at the hole-in-the-wall, the barney in City East station. Ending with a finger hip-hop on the table when he got to his request.

"I want you to say he was here..."

The KitKat on the wall clicked the seconds. The *Gaggia* gulped: otherwise there was nothing else to be heard in there until Renny drew in a breath through his Roman nose that would have filled an ox's lungs.

"You want me to say *what*?"

Dean dropped his voice, said it to the table. "That Clyde was here last night with Sharon. Came with her, went with her..."

"You ask me to say this to the police?"

Dean just about nodded. He couldn't count

on a "yes" coming out.

"Because if I don't say this they'll knock him for snatching cash at the cashpoint?"

Dean's hands did a little out-and-in on the table. He still couldn't lay hold of words.

"But you didn't hang about too much on *why*. Why should I do this thing? Like, I need to know the thinking – why does Dean Romita think his father should risk his good name in this way?"

Dean knew his dad was right to put the squeeze on. Why should he give the law a load of lies? Dean hadn't gone into this feeling right himself; he was giving this shot for his girlfriend, that was all. Which was how it had all come out – the only way it could.

But even as he was thinking how this sounded no more than a load of moonshine, something else came into his head. Suddenly, that man at the hole-in-the-wall, that nerd from Norwich, was back in focus. What he'd said. And, knowing he'd lost, Dean started to get angry again over that rubbish about black crime, and Old Bill giving up on it. His gall rose up as he thought about the man's attitude to people like Sharon and her family. Never mind what Clyde had done – the man had been out of order to say he was typical of every black in the city.

"I'll tell you why I done it. I done it for friendship. I done it out of loyalty. It's people like Sharon and Clyde with the rotten world always against them, and I'm being loyal to them. I'm dead against the racist attitudes of these right-wing prats."

Renny got up, took his time bringing two more *espressos*. With sugar this time, which Dean hadn't noticed missing from the first cup.

"So, Dean Romita wants to fight the racists

with his own prejudice, is that it? His own discrimination?"

"Do what...?"

Renny sipped. "Bending over backwards, doing a plea, giving your *amicos* one law and everyone else something different. That sounds to me as racist as these people who always think the worst. If we want to get somewhere on all this, we've got to go for people *really* being equal. No?"

Cherokee brave sat at feet of Tribal Elder.

He scalded himself on a knock-back of the hot coffee, but he didn't feel it. Renny was right. And he *had* tried, hadn't he?

"No, you wouldn't want me to tell that lie, would you?"

Dean knew that he wouldn't; and being fair, he hadn't, right from the start. This was all a twist of the arm job. He shook his head.

"Which is good between you and me."

Renny got up, took the cups. Dean shivered. The chill of the morning had suddenly come on him through his tee shirt and shorts.

"And quite apart from anything, *figlio*, I don't have to give any alibis to Clyde..."

Dean frowned.

"Your policewoman won't be calling in to see me, unless she wants some breakfast..."

"No?"What had happened? Had Clyde put his hands up? Had he had a shake of the guilts and gone cold on bringing everyone into it? "I don't get you."

Renny came round from behind the counter with his pocket radio.

"It don't matter where Clyde was. If I believe this." And he plonked his little Sanyo on the table as if it were about to answer Dean's question direct.

Chapter Ten

Dean couldn't wait for the next news-on-the-hour to come up, so Renny had to tell him: which he did with his back facing the boy, taking a hung salami and starting to slice it. Which was Sophia's job for later, but in crucial talk it's favourite to have something else to keep your hands and eyes busy.

"Six o'clock, local news..."

"Yeah?" Dean shivered again.

"A young man goes under a taxi, last night.

A skater. A roller ball..."

"Roller blade."

"Got trapped by his boot. Couldn't get free. The boot on the skate."

"When? What time?" Dean's immediate thought – was this Clyde, gone off from the station all strung up and done something sap-brained?

"They don't say what time. But they say how he looks. And not your Clyde, I tell you that." Renny cut fast, busy as a butcher. "When he comes out of hospital, he's under arrest. He's got six hundred and fifty quid in his pocket."

Dean didn't know whether to shout or to swear. *Not* Clyde! What a result! What a let-off for Bro and Sis! That was the first thought. Then, all the aggravation *he'd* had! That was the second. Sharon and Clyde between them owed him a night of his life.

All the same, it was a relief. And with the relief, the floor was starting to chill up through his bare feet. He looked down at his toes, the little ones just on the turn from red to blue. And he wanted his trainers, left under the bed.

Trainers! Now the third thought came. What had the radio said about the thief being trapped by his boots? Where there'd been no ripping boots off and running away – and didn't Dean know that *in-line boots were fixed too solid for that*? Like the shiny red Oxygens in the dream, they were part of the roller blade. While it had been the clamp marks of *old* skates on Clyde's *trainers* he'd seen.

Clyde had old quads, from the look of it – he wasn't a roller-blader at all.

Holy cats! What a clunk he'd been! The rest had looked the same, but he'd put two and two together to make...*nothing*.

"What description did they give?" Dean asked his dad. He just wanted to be sure. Stoneginger certain.

Now Renny put down his knife and turned round. The uncut end of the salami rolled on the board, like something celebrating escaping the chop. He placed his hands on the glass counter to pull full attention to what he was going to say.

"Woollen hat, long black coat, and the skates."

Which still fitted with what Dean had seen and what Clyde had worn – apart from the difference over trainers and boots.

"And he was white. 'White youth', they said." At which Renny turned back and finished off the salami. Chop-chop.

Dean's mouth was suddenly set rigid, like something modelled in gone-off clay. He walked to the door and found the comfort of carpet for his cold feet as he went slowly up the stairs to his bedroom.

White.

He stood with his eyes shut, tried to run it all again in his head – that flash of a figure off the road and onto the pavement; the snatch and the off, back into the traffic. With the woollen hat pulled well down.

And with a deep ache inside, and a groan coming up like wind, he knew what he'd done.

He hadn't seen much of the face, everything had been too quick; and the hands were in wrist-guards. So, the guy could well have been white. But what had Dean's ten-to-one bet been? *His?* Dino Romita's? Mr Race Equality's? Against the facts when the nerd had said "black" he'd gone with it, he'd sided himself with Striped Suit's view of things – he'd been part of the same black prejudice.

And coming from where *he* was at, that was worse, a million times worse.

He was nearly ready for school when the phone rang: City Limits busy with the serious breakfasts now, all steamed windows and the tang of tomato ketchup. And Dean angling through for a piece of toast off his mother to take into the back room.

Renny took the call off the wall. "The Golden Buddha," he told Dean. "His Coke, come this morning!"

Dean clucked in his throat. Would you believe it? All that business last night, and the stuff comes in today! Without the trip with the barrow, he wouldn't have been at the cash-point when the snatch was made. There wouldn't have been any favours being asked by Sharon, no problems with Clyde – and no wild dreams about Clyde and Kwai.

Kwai! Dean had forgotten about Kwai. He looked up at the KitKat.

"I'll go round and barrow it back," he told Renny.

Renny was busy. "Tonight – he's bringing it."

"No, I'll get it."

Renny came round the counter with a breakfast fit for a king, and served it to someone who thought he was just that – jacket draped on shoulders, no arms in the sleeves to crease them, king of Hollywood. Dean got no reply. So he went to the hallway and found the porters' barrow. Well, his dad might run short against the odds, he could have a run on Coke today, couldn't he?

Without the load, he was at The Golden Buddha within ten minutes, tight pavements or not. There was no sense hanging about, never any plus to wasting time. And he needed something to do – too right, he did! He needed to be in and out among people, having to think about poxy things – just to take the slap out of what he'd thought about Clyde.

And perhaps to get Kwai's two cents' worth on what she'd seen last night. Or just her two cents' on anything. Did Coke have the edge on Pepsi? Was this mag a better read than that?

He pushed the bell at the side door. And found himself getting a bit thick in the throat as he waited to see who was going to open it.

It was Mr Ung; who smiled, and asked him in. Dean tripped over the barrow wheel in his tumble to get through the door. Inside, while Mr Ung went for the untouched cases of Coke, he bossed into the back room, ricked his neck to see up the stairs, listened for a voice.

Nothing. So as the Cokes and the thank-yous came, Dean had to ask; otherwise he'd be back in the alley within the half minute.

"Is... er... Kwai about?"

"Kwai?" Her father made her sound like the most distant stranger on Earth. "No. She gone to school. Oh, half hour."

"Right." Of course, she went to posh old All Hallows High, didn't she? A bus ride away – while Dean and Mack only had to walk to theirs. "Well, cheers. My dad said, 'Any time.'"

"OK. Thank you." And the door was closed.

On the outside of which, Dean was back in the alley with three heavy cases of Coke. And no Kwai, and no Mack to help give a push this time. And, yes, no Sharon.

He bumped and steered his fizz back through the streets, trying to go as fast with the full load as he had with the empty.

Because now his aim was to get to school early and see Sharon on her own before classes. To tell her the good news, if she hadn't heard it. And to see her smile.

And he did want to see Sharon's smile. Above all else. Didn't he?